I SAW HIM

AN EYEWITNESS ACCOUNT OF
THE PASSION OF CHRIST

TONYE PERKINS

I SAW HIM:
An Eyewitness Account of the Passion of Christ

By Tonye Perkins
Pictures: Tonye Perkins using AI assisted tools

Copyright© 2025 by Tonye Perkins

Anthonye E. Perkins

56 Hughes Rd. Unit 1091

Madison, AL 35758

go2perksplace@gmail.com

P.S.
PUBLISHING

John 3:16-17

16 *For God so loved the world, that he gave his only begotten Son, that whosoever believeth in him should not perish, but have everlasting life.*

17 *For God sent not his Son into the world to condemn the world; but that the world through him might be saved.* —KJV

"For God so loved the world that he gave his one and only Son, that whoever believes in him shall not perish but have eternal life. 17 For God did not send his Son into the world to condemn the world, but to save the world through him." —NIV

"For God so [greatly] loved and dearly prized the world, that He [even] gave His [One and] only begotten Son, so that whoever believes and trusts in Him [as Savior] shall not perish, but have eternal life. For God did not send the Son into the world to judge and condemn the world [that is, to initiate the final judgment of the world], but that the world might be saved through Him." —AMP

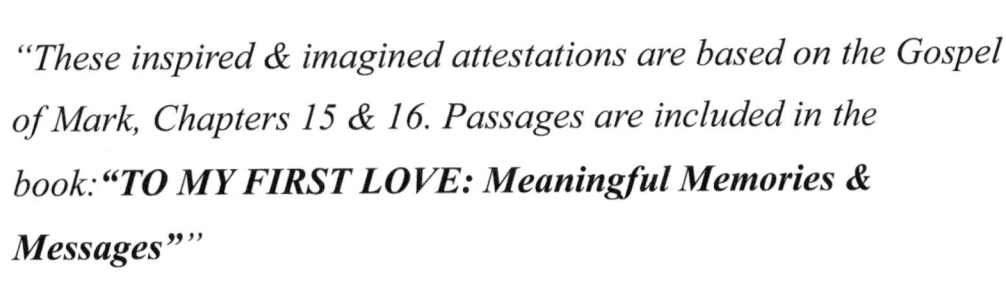

*"These inspired & imagined attestations are based on the Gospel of Mark, Chapters 15 & 16. Passages are included in the book:"**TO MY FIRST LOVE: Meaningful Memories & Messages"**"*

DEDICATION

For the eyes that have seen Him—and hold the vision still.

For the eyes that once saw Him—but let the memory slip.

For the eyes that swear they've never seen Him at all.

This book is for you.

Take a look. Take another look.

And when you see Him this time—

Don't you ever forget.—AETP

PROLOGUE

I Saw Him

I didn't read about Him. Didn't hear it secondhand. Wasn't told by preachers, pamphlets, prophets… or poets.

I saw Him.

With these eyes—Tired, tattered, trauma-trained—
I saw Him. Not just the man. Not just the miracles.
I saw the mercy.

I saw Him when I wasn't lookin'. Felt Him when I wasn't prayin'.
Heard Him in the silence between my sin and my surrender.

I saw Him…

…on the cross…in the dirt…in the eyes of a thief…and in the trembling hands of a mother. I saw Him through storms, behind tears, beneath shame, and beyond death.

I saw Him hold back Heaven while Earth held Him hostage.
I saw Him refuse revenge so He could redeem.
I saw Love hang bleeding… and still choose to forgive.

This book isn't fiction. It's not a fable. It's not a retelling. It's a record of those who were there. Who saw what the world tried to bury. Who can't unsee what they witnessed.

Each page? A testimony. Each voice? A vantage point. Each story? A soul. And when you finish reading…

Maybe you'll see Him too.

TABLE OF CONTENTS

CHAPTER 1

A ROMAN DOSSIER OF WITNESSES

(A RECORD FROM THE PROVINCE OF JUDEA)

ENTRY 1
~PONTIUS PILATE~

"He had no beauty or majesty to attract us to him, nothing in his appearance that we should desire him." — Isaiah 53:2

The Governor's Report: Pontius Pilate
FRIDAY, APRIL 6, 33 A.D.

I SAW HIM TODAY... THE ONE EVERYBODY'S BEEN TALKING ABOUT, THE SO CALLED "PROPHET," THE TEACHER, THE ONE CALLED JESUS...

The chief priests and elders brought him before me. They would not come into the courtroom for fear of being "defiled," yet they acted like a pack of rabid dogs—barking, yelping, snapping at him. And they have the nerve to call themselves men of God.

They woke me from a sound sleep, dragging me from my bed to hear their case. I did not appreciate it, and I quickly let them know. My intent was to pass judgment as rapidly as possible. Because they had disturbed me, I was prepared to hand down the severest punishment they had ever seen.

They brought him bound, as though he were some dangerous animal. Yet he offered no struggle, no resistance, not a single word. I fixed my gaze upon him—the kind of look that causes most men to faint in fear. But when our eyes met, it was as though my heart had been pierced with a centurion's lance. In that moment, I became convinced of his innocence, so noble and majestic was his bearing. I felt compelled to test the charges for myself.

I took him aside, away from the snarling mob, and asked him, "Art thou the King of the Jews?" I asked for two reasons: first, because it was the charge they had brought against him; but secondly, because I wanted to know for myself. I had heard of him. Stories of miracles: of feeding multitudes, healing the sick, even raising the dead. Could he truly be the Jews' long-awaited Messiah? He seemed to read my thoughts. He answered me simply: "Thou sayest it." I understood it to mean, "Do you ask for yourself, or do you ask because others accuse me of it?"

I was unsettled by his answer. The priests pressed their charges with relentless fury, and I asked him again: "Answerest thou nothing? Behold how many things they witness against thee. Art thou the King of the Jews?" He only looked into my eyes. I marveled at his calm, his presence, his inner peace. And in his silence, I became convinced again of his innocence.

In an attempt to save his life, I offered the crowd a choice. Because of their holy festival, I would release one prisoner to them: Jesus, or Barabbas the thief, the murderer, the menace to their society, and the bane of my existence. Surely they would choose Jesus, whose reputation was without fault. Barabbas had only ever brought Roman

wrath upon their own heads. To me, it was an easy choice.
I was wrong.

The religious leaders whipped the crowd into a frenzy. Out of jealousy and envy, they had trumped up these charges against Jesus —but the mob could not see it. It was plain to me that if I did not appease them, those self-righteous "men of God" would stir up unrest, and unrest could jeopardize my political future. I saw through their pathetic little schemes, and I was determined not to be one of their sacrifices.

The crowd screamed for Barabbas. When I asked what should be done with Jesus, they roared back, "Crucify him!"
I was astonished. "What evil hath he done?" I demanded.
They only shouted louder: "Crucify him! Crucify him!"
In the end, it came down to a single choice: I could save the life of this Galilean peasant—or I could save my career. I knew he was innocent, but I owed him nothing. What could he do for me? I was destined for glory. In a fortnight, I told myself, the people would forget his name. No one would remember this man called Jesus.

So I proclaimed: "Let the record show: I, Pontius Pilate, most honorable governor for Rome in the provinces of Galilee and Judea, have had the man Jesus of Nazareth whipped and delivered to be crucified upon a cross." A superscription was placed above his head. To the irritation of the Jewish leaders, it was written in Latin, Greek, and Aramaic:

"This is Jesus, the King of the Jews."

~ PONTIUS PILATE ~
SUPREME GOVERNOR OF GALILEE AND JUDEA.
~ & ~

ENTRY 2
~LUCIUS TIBERIUS~

But he was wounded for our transgressions, he was bruised for our iniquities: the chastisement of our peace was upon him; and with his stripes we are healed.—Isaiah 53:5

The Soldier's Report: A Centurion of Rome
SATURDAY, APRIL 7, 33 A.D.

I SAW HIM TODAY...THE TROUBLE-MAKING GALILEAN FROM NAZARETH CALLED JESUS....

Early this morning, he was brought before His Lordship, Governor Pilate, by a mob of Jewish religious leaders. I was on duty for the night watch. I was given special orders to whip him, which I carried out post-haste. Before the night was over, he would be scourged twice.

Now I've flogged a man or two in my twenty-plus years with the corps. It is said that my cat-o'-nine-tails can be heard meowing when I whip a man. I take pride in my work, and while I'm on duty, there is not a criminal to come through that will not hear my arm purr, or feel the scratch of my whip's claws. Yet tonight was different.

Normally, when a man is about to be whipped, he fights to escape. He swings, kicks, bites, scratches, spits, curses—does whatever he can to gain his freedom. This usually adds to the excitement of the moment and inspires me to really lay it on.

But this one was different. He seemed almost resigned to his fate. Of all the prisoners I have ever seen, he seemed least deserving of his punishment. He appeared to be of royal birth; he carried himself like a man of breeding, yet somehow approachable. In my position, I have served under generals and nobles, but never a man like him, nor one who behaved as he did. And when he looked at you… those eyes… it was as if they said, "I love you. I forgive you for what you're doing to me." Never before has a man so moved me.

Now I am a seasoned soldier, one who has fought in many campaigns, yet his gentleness stirred compassion in me. I lost all the grim joy I normally receive from breaking a man's body and spirit. When it came time for his second scourging, I had not the heart to carry it out. I ordered a detail of men to handle the matter.

Later, the sergeant gave me the details. He said they took the Nazarene to the hall called the Praetorium. Because he was being mocked as the "King of the Jews," the men took extra liberties in their interrogation. The truth is, my men don't like the Jews. They think themselves better than Romans—even though we're the ones who conquered them.

They reported stripping him of his clothing and draping him with a purple robe. They wove together thorn branches into the shape of a crown and jammed it onto his head. My subordinate said the men laughed until they cried as blood spurted from his punctured scalp, running into his eyes, his mouth, his beard. They spat on him and yanked out handfuls of his beard. Surprisingly, their cruelty sickened me.

Then they took a reed, about as thick as a thumb, and beat him about the head, driving the thorns deeper into his skull. They bowed before him in mock worship. Some even "took him," as they sometimes do to a wench, as further humiliation. That's common enough among the lower ranks, though I never encourage it on my watch. The captain of the detail told me that at no time did the prisoner raise his voice in anger, nor did he ever beg for mercy.

When they were done, they pulled the blood-soaked scarlet robe from his shoulders, dressed him again in his own garments, and led him out to be crucified.

At the hill called Calvariae Locus in Latin—"the place of the skull"—and in Aramaic, Calvary, I watched as the men cast lots for his seamless garment, which was of great value. Two thieves were crucified with him, one on either side.

As I stood at the foot of his cross, the mob gathered—pious, hypocritical chief priests, scribes, and Pharisees—taunting him mercilessly:
"If you are the Christ, the Messiah of Israel, come down and save yourself, that we might believe in you. You who said you could destroy the temple and rebuild it in three days—now you cannot even save yourself."

Around the sixth hour, the land grew dark. The darkness around his cross was thick—impenetrable to the eye, even to torchlight. It felt as if I were drowning in ink. Yet in that blackness, I sensed a presence, an entity I cannot explain.

This lasted until the ninth hour, when the Galilean cried out in anguish, "My God, my God, why have you forsaken me?"
Not long after, he cried again: "It is finished!" At that moment, nature itself seemed to rebel. The ground shook like a reed in the wind. Lightning split the sky. Thunder rolled so violently it shook the hill. Later I was told that graves broke open, and the great veil in the Jewish temple was torn from top to bottom.

Standing there on that hill, witnessing all that transpired, I could not help but whisper aloud, "Truly, this man was the Son of God."
No man could endure what he endured, or act as he acted. No man could take such punishment and still look at you with those forgiving eyes—unless he were a god, or at least the son of one. But can one kill a god? And if he was… what becomes of us who did this to him? I wonder.

I did not put my doubts in my official report. Instead, I wrote:
"In accordance with my witness and rank as a centurion in the Army of Rome, I swear before Caesar and the gods, that the report I have given is accurate and true. So say I."

~ LUCIUS TIBERIUS ~
CENTURION
II GARRISON (JERUSALEM), III LEGION
~ & ~

ENTRY 3
~TIBULUM CROSS-BARR~

Surely he hath borne our griefs, and carried our sorrows: yet we did esteem him stricken, smitten of God, and afflicted.—Isaiah 53:4

The Testimony of Tibulum Cross-Barr: The Venerable Order of the Crux Immissa
FRIDAY, APRIL 6, 33 A.D.

I SAW HIM TODAY...THE MASTER, THE CREATOR, THE CRAFTSMAN...

I had been selected to be the instrument of death for any guilty soul who dared oppose the laws of Caesar. I didn't particularly want the job, nor did I like it. Yet I was chosen, while in my prime, by one who could recognize and judge the superlative qualities I possessed. My strength was legendary, my hardiness unequaled. I was considered a prime specimen. After being selected, I was groomed and prepared for duty. In this line of work, you never know who your victim will be until the day of execution.

Of all forms of death, mine was the slowest and most torturous. I wasn't proud of that, nor was I chosen because I loved it. To me, it was just a job—one of many I could perform with excellence. No, I was chosen because I could bear it. But after today...

The guards brought the prisoner into the room with me. I stood by, waiting to perform my dreaded duty. At first I didn't notice him. His head hung low, matted with blood, sweat, and spit. His face was swollen from the crown of thorns pressed into his brow, and from the repeated blows of the guards. His body was limp, his flesh torn raw, exposing muscle and bone. He groaned as they prepared to bind us together.

Just before they tied us, he lifted his head and looked at me. I recognized him—and shrieked in agony.
"No! No! Not him! Not him! Not me! Don't make me do this to him! Dear God in heaven—not to him! Please! Don't let him touch me! I can't do this! I won't do this! Not to him!"

But my cries fell on deaf ears. The guards ignored my pleas. They took heavy rope and lashed us together in what was called the Roman Dance of Death. His blood dripped onto me, seeping into my very pores, burning me from the inside
out. I screamed, but no one listened. No one cared.

They drug us into the street, and the dance began. A mob formed, chanting and jeering as the Son of the Living God and I stumbled through Jerusalem's streets. The road was rough, and more than once I put my full weight upon him. Each time he fell, we both crashed onto the stones, and the mob would kick us, shouting for us to get up, to dance faster.

I begged them to release me. He said nothing. They only laughed and mocked us, spitting on him—and on me. Their spit, mixed with his blood, seeped into my pores and shocked my very frame. I thought I would lose my mind. I tried to roll away, but the fetters were too tight. I was bound.

Finally, when he collapsed and could rise no more, they untied us. I screamed in relief. Free at last! Or so I thought. A guard brought forward a dark, muscular man from the crowd. They ordered him to carry me. He lifted me onto his shoulders as though I were a child. His sweat mingled with Christ's blood, which was already staining me.

This man bore me out of the city, up Golgotha's hill, and laid me down near the summit. It was there that I saw them—three tall, silent companions waiting. Their broad frames could handle the stoutest man. The one in the middle, closest to me, had been weeping. Dark pools marked his rough body. He knew his fate, and like me, his grief drove him near to madness. I hailed him, but he gave no reply. He only sat in silence, grim and waiting.

Then came the moment. They laid me across his back, and with spikes and rope bound us together. In the most hideous act in human history, they placed upon us the battered body of the Christ. And as they hoisted us skyward, all of nature seemed to cry out with us.

I shall never forget this day. For it was on this day the universe witnessed the crucifixion of its Creator. It was on this day the Beloved Son of the Living God was murdered. It was on this day

Jesus, the Christ, took upon his shoulders the sins of the world...
And I—I took upon my shoulders the crucified Christ.

˜ TX-BR ˜
TIBULUM CROSS-BARR,
OF THE VENERABLE ORDER OF
THE CRUX IMMISSA.

CHAPTER 2
THE TESTIMONIES OF
THE HUMAN EYEWITNESSES
(THE RECORD OF THOSE WHO WERE THERE)

ENTRY 4
THE TESTIMONY OF
~SIMON OF CYRENE~

"The Word became flesh and made his dwelling among us. We have seen his glory, the glory of the one and only Son, who came from the Father, full of grace and truth." —John 1:14

The Testimony of Simon of Cyrene
FRIDAY, APRIL 6, 33 A.D.

I saw him today... the one my sons have been following. The one they said was the fulfillment of the promise. The one called Messiah —the Christ.

As usual, I was on my way into Jerusalem. It was nearing the third hour, and I was in a hurry to tend to my business. Then I heard the sound of a large crowd. At first, I thought it might be worshippers gathering for prayers—but the noise was moving away from the city, not toward it. Curious, I quickened my pace.

As I drew closer, I heard the jeering. Taunts. Mockery. Then the words: "Make way for the King of the Jews!" Seeing the Romans in partial battle array, I thought it might be a procession for Herod. But when the line stopped, I found myself face to face with the sight that stole my breath and buckled my knees.

There, beneath the heavy crossbeam of a Roman cross, lay the battered body of a man, drenched in sweat and blood.

The crowd surged around him, spitting, kicking, cursing. Behind him stumbled two other prisoners, but the people hardly noticed them. Their hatred was fixed on him alone.

Horrified, I turned my face away. I asked a nearby soldier, "Who is this man? What has he done that the people despise him so?" The guard sneered, "Him? That's Jesus of Nazareth—you know, the holy man from Galilee."

His answer struck me harder than a blow. My heart tore within me as I looked at him again. And then—he raised his head, and our eyes met. In that moment, I knew who he was. I was convinced beyond all doubt. He was the Son of the Living God! For no man has eyes that pierce through you into your very soul. No man wears such dignity, such nobility, under the weight of such suffering. No man endures the hatred of a mob, yet looks upon them with a love that will not die. I longed to help him. To trade places.

To shield him from their cruelty.

Just then, a rough hand seized my shoulder. I turned—and it was the same soldier I had spoken to. "If you're so interested," he growled, "then maybe you'd like to join in. Get over there, you black knave, and carry that cross!"

I don't know if I ran or if he shoved me, but the next moment I found myself lifting the beam off the Christ. And when I did, he looked into my eyes again. No words were spoken, yet I knew exactly what he was saying: Thank you.

I hoisted that beam onto my shoulders, and I carried it all the way to Calvary. Truth is, I would have carried it around the world if I had to. It was the least I could do—for him.

I stayed there until he died. And at the very moment of his death, I felt the strangest thing. I felt as if, somehow, a weight had been removed from my shoulders. I felt as if I had been given—life.

I will never get over that moment.
I will never forget my encounter with the man from Galilee—
the Son of the Living God.

~ SIMON OF CYRENE ~

ENTRY 5
THE TESTIMONY OF
~THE 3RD THIEF~

"For my Father's will is that everyone who looks to the Son and believes in him shall have eternal life, and I will raise them up at the last day." — John 6:40

Journal Entry: ANON OMIS
FRIDAY, APRIL 6, 33 A.D.:

I SAW HIM…THE MAN IN THE MIDDLE…

He was one of the three; The one in the middle. The innocent one they crucified with my friends—with my compatriots.
I wasn't up there. Not that day—but I should have been!
We ran together—me, him (the one on the left), and the loudmouth on the right who kept mocking that man in the middle. Three sons of the same street, birthed by the same hunger, cradled by the same poverty, formed and fashioned by the same rage. We stole, we scraped, we schemed…anything to not go to sleep with a hollow stomach, a sober mind, or a heavier soul.

We were a tribe, a crew, a band of brothers bound to Barabbas. They called us outlaws, robbers, rebels, bandits. But we weren't thieves, or renegades; we were SURVIVORS…until we weren't.

They caught 'em—my partners, my boys, my "brothers". The Roman's caught them and strung 'em up like street trash, like butchered meat in the market. One on the left. One on the right. And in the middle... Not me...Him! The one we'd heard about. The one who they said walked on water, fed crowds with crumbs, spoke with power and authority, wept with, and over nobodies, and shut Pharisees down with nothing but truth. The same one who, like us, was from the "quarter", the ghetto, the hood.
Jesus of Nazareth!

I watched from the edge of the hill, hood pulled low, heart beating like the hooves of horsemen chasing runaway slaves...or rebel revolters. But it was more than that...it was as if it was pained, pricked, nervous about the feeling that was coming over it.

The loudmouth started in, like he always did. "Man, if you're the Christ, the Messiah, the liberator, then get us down from here! Save us and yourself!" (Same old sarcasm. Same old selfish stench.) But then...my boy—my ride-or-die—flipped the script...he changed the conversation. With blood running down his face, and breath scraping out his lungs, he turned to the middle man, and what he said wrecked me:
"Remember me..." That's it! "Remember me..." He didn't ask for release. He didn't barter a last-minute deal. He didn't ask for proof! He just BELIEVED!

You can bet your last dinara I hadn't seen that coming! I had to get closer to hear the middle man's response. So I took the risk: the risk of being seen, of being recognized and caught, and I snuck closer to the crosses. What I saw and heard…slew me!

The man in the middle looked like he'd been waiting on that moment the whole time.
He turned and looked at my boy with this look of…I don't know… Love? Compassion? Acceptance? Forgiveness! And he said (and I quote), "Today, you'll be with me in paradise."

That's when I completely lost it! That's when I broke! Not in the body…in the soul! 'Cause I knew…I KNEW…that should've been me! I should have been that third man on the cross. I should have been the one hanging on a cross, being
punished for the crimes I committed.

But instead, it was Him. That's when I knew He didn't just die with and for them, He died for us…the liars. The losers. The runners. The lost ones, too ashamed to show our faces at the cross.

I SAW HIM…The SACRIFICE…MY SACRIFICE— The ONE who DIED for ME!
And now…I follow Him.

—ANON OMIS

(FORMER CRIMINAL, CURRENT FOLLOWER OF THE CHRIST)

ENTRY 6
THE TESTIMONY OF
~MARY~
(MOTHER OF JESUS)

"And she shall bring forth a son, and thou shalt call his name JESUS: for he shall save his people from their sins.

Now all this was done, that it might be fulfilled which was spoken of the Lord by the prophet, saying,

Behold, a virgin shall be with child, and shall bring forth a son, and they shall call his name Emmanuel, which being interpreted is, God with us."—Matt. 1:21-23

Journal Entry: Mary, Widow of Joseph,
Mother of Jesus
FRIDAY, APRIL 6, 33 A.D.:

DEAR DIARY,

I SAW HIM TODAY…THE FRUIT OF MY WOMB…

THE DELIGHT OF MY LIFE…MY GIFT FROM GOD…MY

SON…MY BELOVED SON, JESUS.

They never let me forget. Not when I started showing. Not when I said, "It was God." Not when Joseph tried to stand beside me (like he wasn't wrestling too). I know it was a struggle for him. I know he had his doubts, even after he had the visitation. But he stood with me!

Oh, "They" smirked when I passed. Whispered behind my back; Laughed behind "sanctified" synagogue hands; Called MY SON, "that boy"...the one who "didn't look like Joseph (or anyone in his family)."

I raised the Son of God, the light of my life, in the shadows of scandal. Until he started speaking. Until they started following. Until blind eyes blinked, lame legs danced, curved backs straightened, formerly paralyzed people praised, leprous skin smoothed, dead bodies raised, bread banished hunger, and fish fed thousands.

Then... they shut up. I was somebody then, somebody's mama. "The somebody". They whispered different then—still whispers, but now of awe, of admiration, of fear, of liberation from Roman rule, from heathen bondage. And I thought...
maybe that's what God meant when he told me I would be blessed above all women, that my son would be great, and would sit on David's throne! I thought, "Maybe, this is what redemption looks like. My redemption—and his."

But now...Now I'm standing in the last place I ever thought I would be, on top of a hill, at the foot of a Roman cross. I watched them strip my son like a shepherd shears sheep, not his own. I've seen how they beat him within an inch of his life, how they drove spikes in his wrists and feet I played with when he was a baby. I watched as they strung him up, naked as the day I gave birth to him. I watched them treat him like a criminal, bleed him like an animal, like a lamb to be slaughtered, like he meant nothing to nobody.

I listened as they mocked him as a fraud. As they railed on him, and teased him, told him to save himself and come down from that cross! Like a pack of wild hyenas surrounding a wounded lion, I had to listen to their cackling cries and callous jeers.

And every laugh I used to hear behind my back? They're louder now. And the same people who once followed him...They're gone. The same mouths that shouted hosanna at the beginning of this week, shouted ,"Crucify him today, at the end of the week. And those that called him "Rabbi"?
Now call him "Blasphemer."

And I—I'm a woman again. Just a woman. Just "that" woman. Joseph is gone. My son—my only son—my beloved Jesus, is nailed to a tree like a thief—among thieves. And I don't know what to believe anymore. I know what the angel said; I remember the dream, the birth, the boy in the temple, the miracles. I remember...

But what I saw today—my eyes fought my faith—and won. I wanted him to come down. I wanted him to speak, to call down fire, to shake the sky like Moses' God. I wanted him to show them. To prove to them that I was right. That he was right. And all of them were wrong! But all I heard was groaning. All I saw was blood. All I imagined, and dreamt, and hoped for—was dashed!

And yet...Even now... there's this whisper in my womb. Like the one I felt when he first stirred. A whisper that says: "This is not the end. There's more to come." So I stood there, weeping. But watching.

And waiting. Because something tells me (though I barely can see it, or believe it) that though I "saw" him—I'll see him again.

~ MARY ~
(MOTHER OF JESUS)

ENTRY 7
THE TESTIMONY OF
~JOSEPH~
(OF ARIMATHEA)
(Active Member of The Council (Sanhedrin))

"That which was from the beginning, which we have heard, which we have seen with our eyes, which we have looked at and our hands have touched—this we proclaim concerning the Word of life." —1John 1:1-2

Journal Entry: FRIDAY, APRIL 6, 33 A.D.:

Dear Personal Diary,

I SAW HIM TODAY... THE BELOVED RABBI, THE PROPHET, THE PROMISED MESSIAH — CRUCIFIED BEFORE MY VERY EYES!

I saw him strung up on a cross like a freshly slaughtered lamb, like a worthless piece of meat dangling from a hook, suspended between heaven and earth. I watched as filthy flies gorged themselves on the precious blood that oozed
from his torn flesh. I watched as the chief priests, scribes, and Pharisees gorged themselves on his misery. Two swarms circling his suffering: the flies buzzing about his head, the leaders mocking at his feet — both parasites that deserved swatting.

I stood silently as Israel's so-called religious leaders mocked him with devilish delight. They rejoiced that their prey had finally been captured, condemned, and crucified. I watched, and I rebuked myself with anger.

If only I had spoken when the Sanhedrin schemed their plans. If only I had stood when he was dragged before their false trial. If only I had openly believed, openly accepted, openly supported, openly stood with him.

But because of my silence, because of my fear of losing my lofty position, I found myself standing instead at the foot of his cross. It should have been me up there. But it wasn't.

He is dead. I can hardly believe it. Jesus is dead — and my eyes and heart cannot contain the anguish. At the cross, guilt mingled with grief until it crushed my soul. I wept, bitterly and openly.

Yet as I listened to the taunts of the mob, a boldness was born within me. I swore that if I could not honor him in life, then I would honor him in death. Somehow, perhaps, it would make up for my cowardice. So I went to Governor Pilate and begged for his body. To my surprise, the governor agreed.

Back at Golgotha, Nicodemus and I gently received the lifeless body of the Beloved Rabbi, carefully taken down from the cross. Mary of Magdala, Salome, and the other women who had followed him helped us wrap him in the fine linen I had purchased. They anointed him with the myrrh and aloe Nicodemus had brought, and we carried him to my own new tomb. There, we laid him to rest.

Oh Diary... I saw him today. The Master. The Teacher. The Christ. Lying in my tomb. It is an honor I would gladly trade — along with my rank and my reputation — if only I could bring him back to life.

Sleep, Master. Sleep peacefully. May angels guard your body, as I will guard your memory.

~ JOSEPH ~
(OF ARIMATHEA)

ENTRY 8
THE TESTIMONY OF
~MARY~
(OF MAGDALA)

"Then their eyes were opened and they recognized him, and he disappeared from their sight." —Luke 24:31-32

Journal Entry: SUNDAY, APRIL 8, 33 A.D.:

Dear Diary,

GLORY TO GOD! PRAISES BE TO JEHOVAH! I SAW HIM TODAY...

My Beloved Savior. My Redeemer. My Protector. My Deliverer. The one who defended me from the ridicule of the religious leaders, who saved me from the scorn of the scribes, who shielded me from the poisonous piety of the Pharisees. The one who drove away the demons that tormented me, who restored my sense of self-worth, self-respect, and self-esteem. The one who believed in me when I did not believe in myself, who accepted me when others rejected me, who mended my broken heart and filled my empty soul. The one whose head I anointed with perfume and whose feet I washed with my tears.

The one man who loved me more deeply, more completely, more tenderly than any man I had ever known.

Today—I saw Jesus, risen from the grave. And my heart cannot contain the joy. Oh, praise Hosanna!

I was on my way to his grave, carrying the oils and spices for burial. Because he died so suddenly—and because we rushed to place him in Joseph's tomb before the Sabbath began—there had been no time to prepare his body properly. He deserved honor, even in death.

It was early, the dawn just breaking. Each step toward the tomb weighed on me, pressing me deeper into despair. My mind replayed his trial, his torture, his crucifixion, and my tears blurred the path. Then I remembered the great stone at the entrance. Who would roll it away for me? It had taken several men to put it in place. I stopped, uncertain. I almost turned back, but something drew me forward. Even if I could not move the stone, I would wait there until someone came—or die waiting. For what was the point of life, when the Restorer of Life was gone?

When I reached the tomb, I saw the stone had been rolled away. I peered inside. The body was gone. Gone! I screamed. My mind raced. Where is he? Who has taken him? Why? I dropped the oils and spices, frantic, and began running.

I ran as fast as I could back to Jerusalem. Straight to the upper room, where the disciples were hiding. Bursting through the door, I cried,

"Where have you taken him?" "Taken who?" they asked. "The Master —where have you taken him?" They stared at me, bewildered. Between sobs I told them everything.

Peter leapt up and ran without a word, John following close behind. I tried to keep pace but could not.
By the time I arrived back at the tomb, Peter and John were just leaving. Their faces were pale, bewildered. Peter muttered, "They've taken him... they'll say we did it, to bring Rome's wrath on us. We must warn the others." They urged me to come, but I was too weak. My legs gave out. I fell to the ground and wept bitterly.
"My Lord... where have they taken you? Even in death you have no rest." My heart felt like it was being crushed in an olive press.
Then I heard footsteps. I tried to collect myself, head bowed to hide my tears. A man's voice asked why I was crying and who I sought. Thinking he was the gardener, I pleaded: "If you have taken him, tell me where, and I will fetch him."

Then he spoke my name. Just one word: "Mary."
I knew that voice. I turned, my eyes blurred with tears. I wiped them— and there he stood. Jesus. Alive. Radiant. My heart skipped, my breath caught. "Master!" I cried, falling to my knees in joy and reverence. I reached to embrace him, but he gently forbade me, saying he must ascend to the Father. Instead, he sent me with a commission: "Go tell my brethren: I ascend to my Father and your Father, to my God and your God."

Once again, I ran to the city. But this time, my feet felt like they wore the wings of angels. My tears had turned to laughter. My cries became shouts of praise. "Glory to God! My Lord is risen!"

I rushed to the upper room, pounding on the door, shouting, "He is risen! I have seen the Master! He's alive! He's alive!" But they did not believe me. They looked at me with pity, accused me of madness, even of returning to demons.
Peter said, "Woman, thou art crazed." The others shook their heads.

But I know what I saw. I know what I heard.
I am a witness of his resurrection.
And I will tell all who will listen: on this day, at Joseph's empty tomb, I saw the risen Savior.

And though I was the first to behold him, I was not the only one who saw. For even as I rejoiced, a messenger of heaven stood ready to declare the same truth with thunderous voice.

~ MARY ~
(OF MAGDALA)

CHAPTER 3
THE RECORDS FROM THE REALM
(TESTIMONIES FROM THE THRONE)

ENTRY 9
~GABRIEL~
Messenger of the Messiah, Courier of the Crown,
Trumpeter for the Trinity

"But we do see Jesus, who was made lower than the angels for a little while, now crowned with glory and honor because he suffered death…" —Hebrews 2:9

[FOR THE DIVINE RECORD OF THE REALM]

I SAW HIM…MICHAEL…my Captain…my Prince…

I've seen many things…Stars Born…Galaxies Organized & Arranged…Friends turn into enemies; Light turn into darkness… Rebellion and War in Paradise…Heroes Fall…Former comrades cast down like dirty lightning…A being (fashioned by the hands of The Creator) rise from dust, and fall from grace. And the worst thing of all, I saw the creation of the unimaginable—Death!

But nothing—nothing—broke me like that hill. **GOLGOTHA.**

I stood in my place before the throne, peering with the Father through the vastness of space—intently watching the atrocity unfold on the quarantined planet called Earth.

But before that hill…there was…a **GARDEN.**

The place of olives, pressed and crushed—just as He was about to be. I saw Him stumble into the shadows, His disciples—those He called friends—already heavy with sleep. Their eyelids closed, while His heart opened.

He fell to the ground, His face pressed into the dirt of the very earth He formed. And from His lips came words that shook Heaven itself: "Father...if it be possible, let this cup pass from Me. Nevertheless, not My will...but Yours."

The weight of every sin—every betrayal, every murder, every lie, every lust, every hate-filled thought—was pressing upon His soul like the full weight of creation. His sweat became blood, dripping like red rivers, baptizing the soil of Gethsemane.

And The Father looked at me. Just once. No words—just a glance. But I knew what it meant.

"**GO.**"

So I went. Not with the triumph of a trumpet, but with the quiet strength of a brother—a Friend. I descended into that midnight garden, wings muted, voice tender. I knelt beside my Commander. I touched His shoulder—the shoulder that bore the government of worlds—and whispered strength into Him. No sword this time. No shout. Just presence. Just courage. Just a reminder that though the road ahead ran through a cross, it ended in a crown. I gave The WORD, a Word—I told Him of Father's love of & for Him.

He looked at me. Oh, I'll never forget that look! Eyes red with blood and tears, yet steady with resolve. In that gaze was both the weakness of flesh and the power of eternity. He didn't need deliverance; He needed endurance. And so I gave Him what the Father gave me to give.

Then, with a breath that bent the branches overhead, He rose. The Lamb stood ready for slaughter. Alone—but not abandoned. Surrounded by shadows—but filled with the light of Heaven's promise.
And I...faded back into the night. Silent. Watching. Waiting.

THEN CAME THE HILL...

I watched them beat Him. HIM. My Commander. My Captain. My King —Michael, robed in human fragility, bound by the constraints of time and flesh, and the physical laws of that sin-sickened, iniquity-infested, stronghold of satan called Earth. The WORD that created worlds, and spun galaxies...
reduced to groans; His human form, reduced to a bloody mass of flesh; The eyes, through which divinity flashed, dimmed by death.

And I couldn't move! Oh I wanted to; every fiber of my being called out for me to do something! But The Father said:

"WAIT."

Wait?! While they whipped Him? While they mocked Him? While they

shoved spiked thorns into the brow that once wore stars?
WAIT?! HOW COULD I WAIT WHEN THEY WERE
CRUCIFYING MY CAPTAIN?! HOW COULD I WAIT WHEN
THEY WERE KILLING MY CREATOR AND
COMMANDER?!
But…the Father said,

"WAIT."

So I waited. Stood fast. Obeyed. But my sword wept. And when they drove nails through His ankles and wrists, to fasten to the cross His feet and hands—Hands that shaped oceans and softened hearts—hands that created matter, and ALL that MATTERED! …I screamed in silence!

And when they pierced His side? When blood and water flowed? I nearly disobeyed. The throne room shook with my grief, and that of the Father. All of Heaven wept. And all of creation, throughout the universe held its breath.

As we watched the scene in horror & disbelief, I looked to the Father —my heart breaking, my eyes blazing, my body quaking, my wings poised for flight, and fists clenched as tight as my jaws…but the Father's face was resolute. Even with tears in His eyes, He was loving them—even now. Especially now.

And so, I stayed. I waited. And…I watched Him die.

Even when the earth went dark, and convulsed as if from a seizure; Even when rocks were cast off from mountain peaks like leaves from Earth's trees in Fall; Even when graves burst open like ripened fruit… and Raphael split the veil from top to bottom…and Hell roared with false victory…I continued to wait. I waited for three rotations; for three silent eternities.

Then—at long last—He turned to me. THE FATHER, and He said one word:

"GO!"

You've never heard thunder like the cry that left my lungs. I streaked from the Throne Room and headed to earth so fast, light appeared to be standing still. I broke the cords of sound and light just to get to Him. I tore through the atmosphere so hard the devil ducked. Clouds parted. Graves rattled. And the sonic boom caused an earthquake.

I hovered over that tomb like a blazing storm, like a celestial cyclone— And with a voice that shook the stone, scattered the soldiers, and sent shockwaves through the spirit realm, I called out to my Commander:
"ARISE! YOUR FATHER CALLS FOR YOU!"

And He did. Not like a man waking from sleep, but like a King reclaiming His throne. He shook off Death, like dust from His sleeve. Time bowed. Sin trembled. Demons retreated. Satan had a coronary. And I—I wept—with joy. With reverence. With the kind of holy pride no tongue can carry, nor language convey.

I watched Him walk out, with the radiance He wore in the realm. Light itself was blinded by His brilliance. And when He rose—when He ascended—I rose too, along with thousands of my compatriots who met us just outside the Earth's atmosphere, and we flew Home with our Precious Prince.

At the gates to the Holy City we added to our ranks a retinue of cheering cherubs, and we stormed Heaven with a victory parade! You should have seen The Father's face!

Yes, I saw Him. Seated at the right hand of the Father. Crowned, Risen, and Alive…Forever.

I give this testimony freely, of my own accord, and in my Official capacity as:

Gabriel,

~Covering Cherub & 2nd in Command of The Royal Retinue of the Angelic Hosts of Heaven~

ENTRY 10
~ELYON~
THE ANCIENT OF DAYS
The Everlasting Father of Lights

"For God so loved the world, that he gave his only begotten Son, that whosoever believeth in him should not perish, but have everlasting life." — *John 3:16*

"But God commendeth his love toward us, in that, while we were yet sinners, Christ died for us." — *Romans 5:8*

[FOR THE DIVINE RECORD OF THE REALM]

I SAW HIM TODAY—MY SON THE CONQUEROR, MY SON THE LIBERATOR, MY SON, THE LAMB SLAIN BEFORE THE FOUNDATION OF THE EARTH...MY SON—RISEN AND VICTORIOUS!

Before the first star was spoken into place, before the first galaxy spun in its orbit, before eternity itself unfolded—we were together: Christ, Ruach, and Myself. Love was our language, our eternal exchange. A love so fierce, so complete, that it demanded to be shared. And so We chose to create life—sentient beings who could receive it, return it, and walk in harmony with Us. But if they were to be free moral agents—capable of choosing to love or to rebel—then two things were required: Law to guide them, and Grace to redeem them when they strayed.

So, before the foundations of the world, before dust was lifted and kissed with breath, before heaven was peopled with angels, before sin festered in the heart of Lucifer—Love compelled My Son to step forward. "Here am I; send Me." In My heart, before time began, He was already slain (Revelation 13:8).

I was reluctant, but He was resolute. I hesitated, but He was steadfast. I knew if He bore the weight of sin, I would have to turn My face away, and in that turning, I might lose Him. "Yet it pleased the LORD to bruise Him; He hath put Him to grief" (Isaiah 53:10). Justice demanded it, but Love compelled it.

So with unanimous consent of Our Triune counsel, the Plan of Salvation was sealed. My Son would bear the curse, and Ruach and I would pour out an overabundance of Grace. "For God so loved the world, that He gave His only begotten Son" (John 3:16).

When the hour arrived, He laid aside His Divinity once more. First as Michael, Captain of Heaven's Host; then as Jesus, clothed in fragile flesh, walking among a sin-stained earth.

But oh, when Gethsemane came, Our agony began. He prayed; I withdrew. He travailed; I remained silent. The weight of every sin pressed Him into the dust. Angels longed to run to His side— seraphim, cherubim, every host volunteering to strengthen Him—but I forbade them. He had to choose, alone, whether to drink the cup. Only after His will aligned with Mine—"Not My will, but Thine be done

(Luke 22:42)—did I send Gabriel, bearer of light, to strengthen Him, to remind Him of My love and Our plan.

It was the first time I, the Father of All, felt... incomplete. Alone. The first time I tasted separation. The first time I, the Living One, experienced the cold ache of death itself. "My God, My God, why hast Thou forsaken Me?" (Matthew 27:46) was His cry, but it was also Mine. For in that moment, I too was torn, bereft, aching with the grief of hell's separation.

I thought of the lives that would be eternally lost—those who would follow rebellious Satan into the lake of fire. These were they who refused the sacrifice My Son was offering. I thought...and I wept. Only once before, at the fall of Lucifer, had I shed tears. And now... When grief and separation became more than I could bear, I, the Father of Lights, left My throne, cloaked Myself in darkness, and stood before My Son as He hung naked between Heaven and Earth. He could not see Me, nor feel Me, through the shroud of sin that covered Him like a second skin. But I saw Him. I saw the fulfillment of Our plan carried out on a Roman cross. Yes—I saw Him, My Beloved Son, in whom I was well pleased, die before My very eyes.

Then came the silence. Heaven, usually thunderous with song, went still. Seraphim ceased their cry of "Holy, holy, holy" (Isaiah 6:3). Cherubim stilled their wings. Joy was swallowed by grief. All creation held its breath as My Son slept in death. For the first time, I felt bound by time—hours dragging like chains. The Eternal, trapped in waiting; the Timeless, held captive by seconds.

I had never seen Gabriel so tense, so restless. His eyes brimmed with tears, blazing with righteous indignation, waiting for My word—the Word. At the dawn of the first day, I turned to him, and with a nod released him. He needed no more. He flew swifter than thought, splitting time itself, burning the air with his passage.

When he reached the tomb, his glory caused Roman soldiers to faint in terror, and Satan's sentinels to flee in fright. With a flick of his hand, he rolled away the stone, and cried with a voice that shook creation: "JESUS, THY FATHER CALLS THEE!"

Ruach, who had never departed from Him, rushed into the grave on the wings of Gabriel's cry, reached into the depths of death, and reawakened Divinity itself. And to My joy, to My elation, My Son— our Son—rose radiant. Compared to His glory, light became as darkness.

Yet I restrained My joy for a moment, for He lingered long enough to comfort His faithful one, Mary. Then, with Gabriel at His side, He returned—back to His home, back to His family, back to Ruach and Me.

The news of His resurrection raced through heaven like lightning. Seraphim erupted in praise: "HOLY! HOLY! WORTHY IS THE LAMB!" Cherubim, reacting to the call and response, leapt to their stations, crying out in joy, "WORTHY IS HE TO SIT UPON THE THRONE!"

As He approached the Celestial City, surrounded by the angelic host that escorted Him home, the gates trembled with anticipation. The cry went up: "Lift up your heads, O ye gates; and be ye lift up, ye everlasting doors, and the King of glory shall come in!" The angels at the gates, just to hear His name, thundered back, "Who is this King of glory?" And the throng responded in triumph: "The LORD strong and mighty, the LORD mighty in battle!" (Psalm 24:7–8).

This call and response shook eternity. Tears of joy fell like rain. And I...I could not restrain Myself. I rose from My throne and ran to meet Him. We embraced—and we wept for joy. My Son was home!

YES—I SAW HIM! I SAW HIM ASCEND, AND TAKE HIS PLACE AT MY RIGHT HAND—WHERE HE BELONGS!

~YHWH, ELYON~
The Eternal One

CHAPTER 4
HITTIN' HOME
(MY PERSONAL ACCOUNT OF CALVARY)

Putting God Down Part 1:

"My Predicament with Powder" is a deeply personal and theological reflection that begins with the heartbreaking act of euthanizing my beloved cat, Powder. Through raw emotion and vivid memory, I draw a startling spiritual parallel between the mercy that compels us to end a creature's suffering and the divine mercy that compelled God to allow His own Son's death on Calvary. What begins as a private moment of grief unfolds into a profound revelation about compassion, loss, and the painful cost of redemption—reminding us that love, even when it breaks our hearts, is often the very hand of God at work.

Putting God Down, Part 2:

"I'm Tired of Tears" brings the emotional journey full circle. What began as the painful goodbye to a beloved pet becomes a profound meditation on divine sorrow—the agony of a Father watching His Son die to save an ungrateful world. In this heart-wrenching reflection, I wrestle with grief, mercy, and the unbearable cost of love, inviting you to imagine not only Christ's suffering, but the Father's tears. Through vivid imagery, poetic lament, and spiritual honesty, this piece asks the haunting question: **"Who wipes away the tears of God?"**

PUTTING GOD DOWN 1

"My Predicament with Powder"
(EXCERPT FROM MY BOOK, "TO MY FIRST LOVE")

On June 21, 2016, my wife and I had to euthanize our beloved cat, Powder. The previous November, we had to do it to her "Baby" Portia. (Portia was 17 going on 18, and Powder was 16 going on 17.) We were still feeling the pinch from Portia's ordeal when we were confronted with Powder's situation.

T.P.P., Talcum Powder Perkins. My wife used to say that Powder was my cat, because he would follow me around like a devoted dog; he would also look out and call for me when I was gone. And, I was just about the only person who could lift (and whom he would allow) to hold him. When I was home, I couldn't move for him. He was my son, and he didn't mind letting me, and the world know it. With the loss of Portia, Powder became my wife's constant companion while I was at work. If it sounds like I'm eulogizing him…well, I guess I am.

I C it™ with TONYE
"Putting God Down Prt.1"

Anywho, Powder's health had been steadily getting worse, so, out of mercy and compassion, my wife and I made the hard call to have him...put to sleep. The process took place at the vet's office; I held him as she gave him the two drugs that ended his life. (It still brings tears to my eyes when I think about it.) The first shot was an anesthetic, which put him to sleep, and the second was a powerful drug that stopped his heart. (I believe it's the same drug cocktail used to execute prisoners.)

It was eerie and a little discomforting to watch the process, as well as being a part of it. (After all, wasn't I the one holding him in my arms as he breathed his last breath, and that animation we know to be the breath of life, slowly left his body?) (Ohhh but I can tell you we're going somewhere with this.)

That whole situation made me more keenly aware of what happened in Orlando, Florida when a crazy man, hyped-up on sin entered Pulse Nightclub and began killing people. I thought of the horror and panic people must have felt as they watched people die, as they witnessed individuals taking their last breaths, and the animation we call LIFE slowly, and in some cases, violently leave their bodies. I also developed a deeper understanding of how close to death all of us are; how, in a moment, in an instant, in half of a blink of an eye, one can be here...and then gone.

When my wife and I first walked into the vet, we were both kinda hoping she would take a look at Powder and tell us, "Oh no, he's got some more life left in him. Here's a magic pill, give it to him (and us) and he'll (we'll) miraculously recover from the effects of (sin) age, poor health, grief from the loss of a lifelong companion... you know, the stuff we all go through on a daily basis. (We both were kinda hoping, but mostly praying, that we would be turning around and taking our beloved son back home, and that everything would be fine.)

Yeah, we were hoping that, but secretly, waaaay down deep, we knew that wasn't gonna be the case, that (sin) sickness and disease had gone too far; had taken hold of our "beloved son" a little too strongly, and the only course, and recourse we had, was to PUT HIM DOWN, to allow the "remedy" to do its job and end his life.

IT WAS HEARTBREAKING AND GUT-WRENCHING! There were moments during the process when I wanted to scream out, "NO! NO! STOP! STOP! I DON'T WANT TO GO THROUGH WITH THIS...IT'S TOO HARD; IT'S TOO PAINFUL; IT'S TOO DEVASTATING FOR ME! LET'S STOP AND TAKE A STEP BACK; LET'S RELOOK AT THIS THING! EVERYBODY JUST STOP AND TAKE A BREATH! But, because of MERCY, I couldn't; because of COMPASSION I had to let him go; because I knew what the final outcome would be, I had to let things take their course.

I tried to play tough; I tried to be strong, but man I'm telling you, I was DYING inside; I was losing my mind with grief; my skin was crawling and it took everything in me not to run out of that place with my (sin) sick beloved son!

I'm telling you, the situation of us having to put our cat down reminded me of the PAIN, the MISERY, and the profound sense of loss the victims, the survivors, and the families of the victims of the Pulse Nightclub Shooting (and all the mass murders since then) were/ are going through. How can they be consoled? How can they be comforted? How can they be reconciled to their present reality?

But much more than the situation of taking our son to the vet and participating in his life being taken, reminded me of the grief I caused Elohim, more than 2000 years ago! It helped me better understand my role in the crucifixion of Christ; it was because of MY actions He took on the infection, the disease called sin, and the universe had to stand by as witnesses, as Jesus the Christ, the Beloved son
to the Most High God, was put down by the hands of man, and the will of His father. It was MY and YOURS, that the Father had to participate in an act so violent, so extreme, so heartbreaking, so gut-wrenching, that it will be talked about throughout eternity!

I got a minuscule sense of the anguish the Father felt, as He held His son in His…Mind, and watched the doctors of death do their thing; I better understood the inner turmoil, and the ambivalence the Father may have felt, as he watched His son draw His last breath, and the animation we call life, slowly leave His body; I was finally able to get my mind around these things called COMPASSION and MERCY.

"For God so loved the world, that He took His Only Begotten Son…[to the "Doctors of Death", and allowed them to put Him (His

Beloved Son) down (like a dog/cat in a kennel)], that whosoever... [takes the time to really see what happened, to really investigate the crime, to really confront the massacre, and the madman who did it, and turn away from that homicidal, mass-murdering maniac], believes in/on Him (Christ) [completely surrendering themselves to the true, and living God], shall not have to worry about the second/final death, but will live eternally."

* * *

"Behold, what manner of love the Father hath bestowed upon us... [That we are not taken to the Universe's Vet (professionally known as "Justice"), and put down like the dogs we can be, and actually deserve, but instead]...that we should be called the sons of God..."

Lord why you love me, I'll NEVER know!
But, I do appreciate it...and YOU.

PUTTING GOD DOWN 2

"I'm Tired of Tears"

(EXCERPT FROM THE BOOK, "TO MY FIRST LOVE")

Previously, I spoke with you about having to put my beloved cat down. I told you of my anguish and ambivalence, of my discomfort and distress at being a participant in the humane murder of my surrogate son — my beloved pet, Powder.

And, thanks to the Father of Lights, I was able to make a connection between my personal participation in that state-sanctioned act of mercy killing and my public participation in the state-sanctioned murder of Jesus the Christ — the half-human Herald of Heaven, the singular Savior of the Celestial City-State, the undisputed Darling of Divinity.

Through my experience with Powder, I was able to glimpse what God sees — and what God feels — daily: the results of sin, the outcome of iniquity.

"Putting God Down Prt.2"

As I held Powder — my pet, my companion of sixteen years, my baby, my son — he looked up at me with both trust and confusion. He'd been to that place before, and it had often included pain. I imagined him thinking: "Oh yeah, you're telling me everything's gonna be all right, but this place… this is a place where they hurt me, where I suffer discomfort. So why are we here again?" That's what I "imagined" he thought—('cause that's what I would've thought).

Then they took him in the back, gave him the IV, and brought him back to us "to comfort" and spend our last moments together. I imagined him looking at me and thinking: "Yo Dad, what's up? Why are you letting them do this to me? I'm ret-ta-go! Tell them to pull this thing out of my leg and let's blow this joint."

But, nooooo. I just held him, and pretended, whispering the same old reassurances: "It's okay, buddy. I love you, man. Things are gonna work out. You're a good boy." But, deep down, both of us knew they wouldn't. I reflected on Powder, our relationship. As he's looking at me with these tired, inquisitive eyes, I imagine him saying again, "Dad, what are we doing here? How did things get so horribly bad that we have to end up in this place?" And I'm side-stepping the question with my, "Hey Buddy Boy, it's okay. I love you man. You're a good boy." I'm telling you, I WAS IN HELL—THAT THING HURT!

But, I couldn't bear to see him suffer anymore. I couldn't bear to watch him have those days where every movement was excruciating. Where every fiber of his being must have screamed in pain. Where agony lived in his eyes and was etched on his face. And as I looked down at him, I thought about man's inhumanity to man, the suffering and degradation man can callously cause his neighbor.

And, I thought of another picture — Israel at the temple, holding the family lamb, looking into its eyes while the priest's knife slit its throat, and the blood and animation we call Life, slowly drains from the "victim's" body. The sacrifice was supposed to remind and deter us from constantly committing sin. It wasn't just ritual; it was designed to make sin visible, visceral, unforgettable.
And yet — how quickly we forgot—and forget.

Then came the moment. The executioner, I mean doctor walked in. As I held him in my arms, my heart pounding, she administered the drug that would take his life. I held him as he drifted into nothingness, as life — that breath of God — slipped away, and he died the "second" death.

Quickly, I realized: what I experienced was more than what the Heavenly Father received with His own Son. I at least held my boy in my arms, whispering my love as he left
me. The Father had to stand by, cloaked in darkness, hiding His horror, His pain, His face, unable to comfort His Beloved Son in that final moment. How twisted is that?

What did the Father go through for us? What depths of pain tore His heart as He watched part of Himself die upon that cross? Oh, yes, He knew resurrection was coming — but imagine His anguish in the moment. Imagine my story with Powder, multiplied by infinity. Imagine God having to put his own son down to save us, a rebellious race of haters, murderers, and no-gooders. Think about the trauma He experienced when His first created son turned his back, and the backs of 1/3 of the angels, on God? Feel His heartache as He forcibly put his son out of His home because he was too dangerous—too much of a threat to the peace and stability of the home.

And THAT pain, those tears were just the beginning of His anguish—a foretaste of what He would feel when mankind fell, Calvary became a reality, and the Final Judgment and punishment of the wicked is exacted.

So, this begs the question:

Who Wipes Away the Tears of God?

WHO WIPES AWAY THE TEARS OF GOD?

Who wipes away the tears of God?
Who heals His broken heart?
Who wipes away the tears of God
when His heart's being torn apart?
Who laments the loss of unsaved souls
at the moment of sin's demise?
Who has the heart or wherewithal
to wipe the tears from God's eyes?
Who eases the angst of God's agony
as He ignites the fires of hell?
Who comforts the Lord eternally
as He remembers the souls who fell?
Who fills the hole in God's sanctified soul
as He mourns Lucifer's death?
Who bears the burden of grief untold
when God's loss leaves Him pained and bereft?
Who'll wipe away the tears of God?
I fear, there's not one we can find.
Who'll wipe away the tears of God
as He mourns the loss of mankind?

Folks — I don't know about you, but I am tired.
Tired of heartache and pain.
Tired of sickness, death, and dying.
Tired of trials, troubles, and tragedies.
Tired of mishaps, mayhem, and murder.
Tired of watching the devil harass and hound my heart, whip and
wound my butt, destroy and devour my joy.
Tired of seeing neighbors, friends, family and folks overtaken,
overrun, and overcome by disaster, devastation, disease and death.
Tired of watching them lose their bearings, footing, faith and future,
Tired of sin crushing souls beneath its audacious, enormous and
unbearable weight.
Tired of the devil playing champ while we play the chumps.

I'm tired.
Are you?

EPILOGUE
~THE FINAL WITNESS~

For The Record:

The records have been given.

The testimonies have been spoken.

From Rome's tribunal, to the streets of Jerusalem, to the courts of heaven itself —

Every voice has borne witness.

Each account, whether from ruler or soldier, stranger or saint, angel or Almighty, has pointed to the same truth:

He was seen. He was heard. He was given.

From the governor who washed his hands,

to the soldier who stained his,

from the timber that bore his weight,

to the stranger who carried his burden,

from the thief who gained relief,

To the mother who lost it,

From the man who fought with his guilt,

To the woman who became guilt-free,

From the angel who strengthened him,

to the Father who gave him...

All have spoken. All bore witness. All Saw Him.

And now...So Have You.

WHEN DEATH COMES CALLING
(LEAVE DEATH NOTHING)

When death comes calling,
leave it the empty, inconsequential carcass of your essence,
the dribble, dregs and dross of your dreams,
let death glean, a withered wisp of your wisdom;
when death comes for you (as only it can do),
leave it the scant, silted slag of your soul,
and the burned out husk of your being.

When you die—for ALL must go—
leave death the frivolous grounds and granules of your gusto,
the rationed-out remnants of your reason;
and in your final season,
leave death the meager minutiae of your memories.

When death comes a calling,
leave it the Insignificance of your intellect,
the selected, skimpy sediments of your smallness;
leave for none to see,
the undesirable dross of your delinquency.

When death comes to take you away,
leave no wasted words, or unspoken accolades,
no unsaid notions, endorsements, honors or emotions,
but leave it the lasting silence of your last breath.

When finally it's your time,
after death has raced you, and chased you,
to the finish line,
leave ole death, completely out of breath,
stuttering, and stammering, cussing and crying.

And as death comes to claim you,
you must, let its disappointment and disgust,
reverberate throughout eternity;
let it steal the vacant, voided shell, of a life so well lived,
there's nothing left worth taking.

When death comes calling for thee,
let your only regret be,
It waited too long,
and didn't come sooner.

~Tonye Perkins~
2025

BONUS MATERIAL

FOR GOD LOVED SO THE WORLD,
THAT HE   GAVE…

NEVER TURN BACK

ABOUT THE AUTHOR

(Photo by Chris McNish, SweetGap Photography)

Anthonye Earle "Tonye" Perkins is a writer, poet, media producer, and visionary who has spent a lifetime weaving stories through word, sound, and image. From the streets of Berkeley, California, to studios, classrooms, pulpits, and stages across the nation, Tonye has used his gift of language to make people laugh, cry, reflect, and remember. His creative works blend spoken word, satire, theology, and raw storytelling into a voice that is both unapologetically urban and profoundly spiritual.

With decades of experience as a videographer, director, and trainer, Tonye has produced projects for schools, corporations, churches, and communities. His work in broadcast and video production, along with his radio program *Sunset 2 Sunset*, have positioned him as a trusted creative force whose mission is to inform, inspire, and ignite change.

But beyond his craft, Tonye embraces his calling as an **Empath Warrior**—one who feels deeply, stands fiercely, and speaks truth with compassion and courage. Through his writing, he channels both empathy and fire: the sensitivity to understand brokenness, and the boldness to confront it. His words are weapons of healing and instruments of hope.

In his books—*This Black Skin, Papa Goose's Gospel & Other Rappers' Rhymes*, and *To My First Love*—Tonye invites readers into spaces where faith wrestles with doubt, joy collides with pain, and God's love breaks through it all. *I Saw Him* continues that journey, testifying to the Christ who suffers, saves, and reigns.

Tonye lives with the conviction that art is ministry, that storytelling is soul work, and that every page is an altar. As an Empath Warrior, he writes not only to be heard, but to help others see—and never forget —the One who first saw us.

HOW TO CONTACT THE AUTHOR:

Tonye Perkins
56 Hughes Rd., Unit 1091
Madison, AL 35758

EMAIL: go2perksplace@gmail.com
FB: Anthonye Perkins
BLUESKY: aetp.bsky.social
IG: earletonye
YOUTUBE: Tonye Perkins
(@tonyeperkins4715)
Jes'Us Productions
(@MrTonyeP)
WEBSITE: perksplace.net

OTHER WORKS
BY THE AUTHOR

This Black Skin is a soul-stirring testimonial word through poetry and narrative. The collection empowers the will to push forward into the recognition of the pain placed on the black body because of skin color. The collection compels reflection. The questions posed are rhetorical and interrogative. Anthonye Perkins implicitly asks questions demanding one answer: "When will the black body be free of the bondage of abuse because it lives in "this black skin?" —Dr. Ramona Hyman

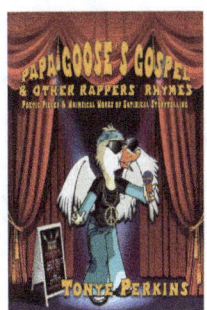

Papa Goose's Gospel & Other Rappers' Rhymes is a bold fusion of spoken word, satire, and raw story-telling. With biting wit and lyrical rhythm, Tonye Perkins delivers social critique and poetic commentary that will make you laugh, cry, nod in agreement, and wrestle with truth. Written with the cadence of the street and the insight of the Spirit, this collection is a rhythmic masterpiece of gospel and grit—thought-provoking, entertaining, and unforgettable.

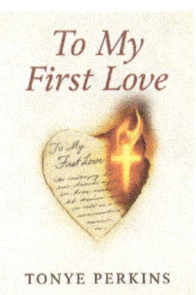

To My First Love is a raw, poetic journey back to the heart of Christ—the One who loved us first. Blending spoken word rhythm with intimate prose, Tonye Perkins writes as an Empath Warrior, exposing struggle, longing, faith, and redemption with honesty and fire. This collection is both testimony and invitation: to remember, to return, and to rediscover the relentless love of God that heals, confronts, and never lets go.

In a world suddenly reshaped by a pandemic, ordinary moments became extraordinary stories. **COVID CREATIONS** is a collection of short tales that capture the ironies, heartbreaks, humor, and hope that defined our 'new normal.' From masked encounters and misunderstood strangers, to auctions for survival and unexpected jackpots, these stories explore the human condition in a time of global crisis. Welcome to a universe where the everyday got flipped upside down- and where every pause, pivot, and punchline hits just a little differently.

FOR YOUR ENCOURAGEMENT

Christ's Sacrifice & Love

- **Romans 8:32** — *He that spared not his own Son, but delivered him up for us all, how shall he not with him also freely give us all things?*
- **Galatians 2:20** — *I am crucified with Christ: nevertheless I live; yet not I, but Christ liveth in me: and the life which I now live in the flesh I live by the faith of the Son of God, who loved me, and gave himself for me.*
- **Ephesians 5:2** — *And walk in love, as Christ also hath loved us, and hath given himself for us an offering and a sacrifice to God for a sweet-smelling savor.*
- **Hebrews 9:28** — *So Christ was once offered to bear the sins of many; and unto them that look for him shall he appear the second time without sin unto salvation.*

Reconciliation & Forgiveness

- *Colossians 1:20–22* — And, having made peace through the blood of his cross, by him to reconcile all things unto himself... in the body of his flesh through death, to present you holy and unblameable and unreproveable in his sight.
- *1 Peter 2:24* — Who his own self bare our sins in his own body on the tree, that we, being dead to sins, should live unto righteousness: by whose stripes ye were healed.

- *1 John 2:1–2* – If any man sin, we have an advocate with the Father, Jesus Christ the righteous: and he is the propitiation for our sins.

Victory & Encouragement

- **Hebrews 12:2** — Looking unto Jesus the author and finisher of our faith; who for the joy that was set before him endured the cross, despising the shame, and is set down at the right hand of the throne of God.
- **1 Corinthians 15:57** – But thanks be to God, which giveth us the victory through our Lord Jesus Christ.
- **2 Corinthians 5:21** – For he hath made him to be sin for us, who knew no sin; that we might be made the righteousness of God in him.
- **Revelation 1:17–18** – Fear not; I am the first and the last: I am he that liveth, and was dead; and, behold, I am alive for evermore, Amen; and have the keys of hell and of death.

NOTES/THOUGHTS

HAVE YOU SEEN HIM?

_____

_____

_____

_____

_____

_____

_____

WHEN?

_____

_____

_____

_____

_____

_____

WHERE?

_____

_____

_____

_____

_____

_____

HOW?

WHAT DID YOU SEE?

WHAT DID YOU HEAR?

WHAT DID YOU THINK?

_____
_____
_____
_____
_____
_____
_____

WHAT DID YOU FEEL?

_____
_____
_____
_____
_____
_____
_____

HOW DO YOU FEEL?

_____
_____
_____
_____
_____
_____
_____

WHAT IS YOUR PRAYER?

WHAT ARE YOU GOING TO DO?

WITH WHOM WILL YOU SHARE?

~LET ME KNOW HOW THIS BOOK IMPACTED YOU~
(USE THE CONTACT INFO ABOVE)

www.ingramcontent.com/pod-product-compliance
Lightning Source LLC
Chambersburg PA
CBHW051840020726
47502CB00005B/1881